A Catalogue record for this book is available
from the British Library

ISBN 978 0 340 98149 8 (HB)
ISBN 978 0 340 98155 9 (PB)

Typeset by
Tony Fleetwood

Printed and bound in Great Britain by
Clays Ltd St Ives plc, Bungay, Suffolk

The paper and board used in this book is a natural recyclable product made
from wood grown in sustainable forests.

Hodder Children's Books
a division of Hachette Children's Books
338 Euston Road, London NW1 3BH
An Hachette UK company
www.hachette.co.uk

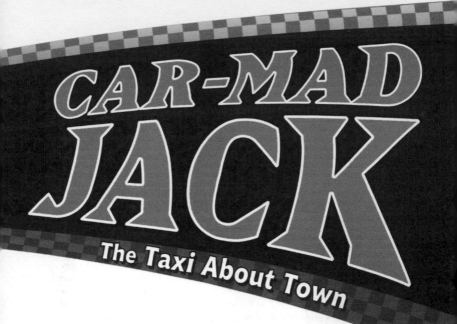

CAR-MAD JACK
The Taxi About Town

Written by
JENNY ALEXANDER

Illustrated by
MARK OLIVER

Hodder
Children's
Books

A division of Hachette Children's Books

Written by
JENNY ALEXANDER

Illustrated by
MARK OLIVER

· CHAPTER 1 ·

Nico was having a tantrum. He kicked and screamed when Mum tried to get him into his jacket. As soon as she got one arm in, the other one popped out. He kicked and screamed when she strapped him into his car seat. He kicked and screamed all the way to the car supermarket.

Jack and Amber had to put their hands over their ears!

As soon as they arrived, Jack jumped out. Dad was waiting outside on the forecourt.

'What's the matter with Nico?' asked Dad.

They could hear him screaming even though the car windows were closed. They could hear him even when the car drove off down the road.

'He's lost Crocky,' said Jack.

Dad groaned. 'Oh, dear,' he said.

Nico took Crocky everywhere. He played with Crocky and cuddled him so much that most of his green fur had rubbed off. Crocky had lost his shape and gone baggy and limp. He didn't really look like a crocodile any more. He looked more like a brown sausage with feet. But Nico loved him.

'We searched everywhere,' said Jack. 'But we couldn't find him.'

'Don't worry,' said Dad. 'Nico will be all right. He loves his Saturday mornings shopping with Mum. He'll soon forget about Crocky.'

Jack nodded, but he didn't really believe it.

Dad said, 'I've got a meeting this morning, so I've asked Uncle Archie to keep an eye on you.'

'Cool!' said Jack.

They walked round to the back of the showroom and Dad watched Jack cross the yard. Uncle Archie came out of the workshop to greet Jack. He waved to Dad, and Dad went off to his meeting.

Uncle Archie was a bit older than Dad. He was also a bit fatter. This was probably because of the big bag of doughnuts that Brian the mechanic brought in every day.

Uncle Archie wore blue overalls, not smart suits like Dad. His hair was straggly, not neat like Dad's. But you could tell that they were brothers. They both had the same smiley eyes.

'Hello, Jack,' said Uncle Archie. 'Dad tells me you're going to hang out with Brian and me this morning.'

Jack nodded. He peered into the workshop to see what Uncle Archie and Brian were working on. It was a Ford Escort. There were usually two or three cars parked outside the workshop waiting to be checked and cleaned before they went on sale. But there weren't any cars waiting today.

'Sorry, mate,' said Uncle Archie, seeing Jack's disappointment. 'It's a bit quiet out here this morning. But you never know what might come along.'

Just as he said that, a shiny black taxi drove into the yard! The driver parked and got out. He was wearing a yellow sweater with red diamonds down one side, and a gold watch as big as a biscuit. He strode across the yard and shook Uncle Archie's hand.

'Morning, Archie!' he said. He had a big booming voice. 'Can you take a look at my cab this morning? The engine's running a bit hot.'

'No problem, Sam,' said Uncle Archie. 'I'll do it when we've finished the Escort.'

Jack really wanted to play in the taxi but he wasn't allowed to play in other people's cars. He was only allowed to play in the

cars that were for sale, because those ones
belonged to Dad and Uncle Archie.

Sam seemed to notice Jack for the first
time.

'Who have we got here?' he asked.

Uncle Archie said that Jack was his
nephew, and he was mad about cars.

'Everyone calls him Car-mad Jack,' he
added.

'I was mad about cars when I was your

age,' said Sam. 'That's why I became a taxi driver.'

Sam told Jack that being a taxi driver was the best job in the world because you got to drive around all day long and meet lots of interesting people. But it could be stressful too.

'There are three things that can stress out a taxi driver,' he boomed. 'Can you guess what they are?'

'Um ...' Jack thought hard.

'OK, number one – traffic jams,' interrupted Sam. 'Number two – rude passengers. Number three – people leaving things in your cab.'

'Does that happen a lot?' asked Uncle Archie.

'You'd be surprised,' nodded Sam. 'Most

of the time it's just things like shopping bags or sweets, but sometimes it might be a laptop or a bracelet or a bank card. You have to decide whether it's important enough to chase half way across the city trying to find the person and give it back.'

Uncle Archie laughed. 'That does sound stressful!' he said. 'How do you stop yourself getting wound up?'

'I have this little thing I say to myself – "Keep calm, keep polite." It seems to work,' said Sam.

He gave the keys to Uncle Archie, and shook his hand again. Jack looked longingly at the taxi.

'Do you ever play in the cars?' asked Sam.

Jack nodded. 'Yes, but only the ones that are for sale, and I always stick to the rules.'

'What are the rules?' said Sam.

Jack said, 'No feet on seats, no food or sweets, no horns or buttons or brakes.'

'Those are the same rules I had when I was a boy and I used to play in my Dad's car,' said Sam. 'You can play in my taxi if you like, since you know the rules.'

Jack was overjoyed! As soon as Sam had gone, he and Uncle Archie went to look at the taxi. It was shiny black on the outside, with a 'Taxi' light on the top.

'If the light is on, you know the taxi is empty,' Uncle Archie said. 'The driver turns it off when he's got a passenger.'

He opened the wide back door. There was lots of room inside. As well as the big

back seat, there were two flap-down seats
facing backwards. There was a barrier
between the driver and passengers. It had
a glass panel with an intercom, so that the
driver and passengers could talk to each
other.

The seats and floor were grey, but there
were red safety handles and notices. One
said, 'The law requires you to wear your

safety belt.' Another one said, 'Please
remember to take your belongings with
you.'

Uncle Archie opened the driver's door
and Jack climbed in. It wasn't like a
normal car. The passenger side had no seat,
just a space for holding luggage. There was
a meter on the dashboard that showed how
much money the ride was costing. There
was a switch for the intercom.

Jack couldn't wait to be on his own. He would pretend to be a taxi driver. He would keep calm even if the traffic was really bad. He would be polite even if the passengers were really rude.

Uncle Archie stepped back from the taxi.

'I'd better go and help Brian with that Ford Escort,' he said. 'Happy driving, Jack!'

· CHAPTER 2 ·

Jack wondered, 'Where shall I start my taxi-driving adventure?'

Where would you usually see a London taxi cab? Jack suddenly remembered where he had seen lots of taxis. There was a long row of them outside Paddington Station the day he and his family took the train to see the Christmas lights in Oxford Street.

He remembered all the people rushing through from the trains to catch a taxi. There was a bald-headed man in a suit and shiny shoes. There was a smart young woman with a laptop. There were two young men carrying huge rucksacks on their backs. There was a gaggle of giggly girls who looked like pop stars in their twinkly party clothes.

Jack put his hands on the steering wheel. He imagined that his taxi was at the front of the line outside Paddington Station. He was wearing his taxi-driver jacket. He had his taxi-driver badge on. Lots of people were striding out of the station towards the taxi rank. Who would get into his cab?

Jack's first passengers were a family on a day trip. He jumped out to open the door for them. There was a boy who looked about eight, a girl who looked about five and a toddler in a buggy. They all looked happy and excited. The mum lifted the toddler out of her buggy. The dad folded up the buggy and Jack put it in the luggage space.

There was plenty of room for them all inside. The mum and dad sat with the toddler on the big back seat. The children sat facing them on the fold-down seats. The dad said, 'Natural History Museum please, driver!' Jack the cab-driver started the engine once they'd all fastened their seatbelts.

Jack had the intercom on so he could

hear the family in the back. He learned that the children were called Mitch, Molly and Little Min. They were talking about all the things they were going to see on their day-trip to London. After the Natural History Museum they were going to the Tower of London.

'I'll take a picture of you standing next to the beefeaters who guard the tower,' said the Dad.

'Do you think they'll let us have some of their beef?' asked Molly.

Cab-driver Jack smiled to himself. He had made the same mistake the first time he went to the Tower of London. He

thought that the beefeaters did nothing but eat meat all day long. Come to think of it, if that wasn't what they did, why were they called beefeaters?

'I haven't got time to think about that now,' cab-driver Jack told himself. There was lots of traffic so he had to keep his mind on the road. Other cars kept weaving in and out, pushing in front of Jack, tooting their horns. But Jack didn't feel stressed – he was used to driving in London traffic.

There were lots of crossings with traffic lights, but Jack didn't mind if he had to stop at a red. He was happy to have a chance to look around at the bright shop windows and the people walking by.

Once or twice, someone couldn't be

bothered to wait at a crossing and ran out
in front of the cars, making the drivers slam
on their brakes. Some drivers swore and
shook their fists, but cab-driver Jack just
slowed down to let them cross. He was used
to people being in a rush.

They arrived at the Natural History Museum. Cab-driver Jack jumped out. He fetched the buggy from the luggage space and opened the door for the family. They waited on the pavement while the dad paid Jack.

Molly was tugging at her mum's sleeve, trying to get her to notice a fat pigeon pecking at an old sandwich on the pavement. Mitch was fussing because he couldn't work out how to take a picture of it with his new mobile.

Little Min was crying. Her mum was struggling to get her into her buggy.

'She's just fed up because she was enjoying riding in your taxi,' said the dad.

Jack smiled. 'She'll cheer up when she sees all the amazing things in the museum.'

Cab-driver Jack said goodbye to the family. He switched the 'Taxi' light on to show that he was free again. Then he started to drive off.

'That was easy!' he thought. 'I didn't run into any traffic jams and my passengers were not rude. I didn't feel stressed at all!'

Jack was thinking maybe his first ride had been a bit too easy when he got a call on his mobile.

'I need a cab to pick up a very famous person from The Ritz hotel right now,' said the caller. 'Are you free?'

Oooh ... this could be exciting – a very famous person! Who could it be?

The caller said that the very famous person had to be at the Film of the Year Show in half an hour. Jack had seen the Film of the Year Show on the News. All the film stars got out of their cars and walked down a long red carpet. Cameras flashed. Newsmen jostled.

'Yes, I'm free!' said Jack. 'I can be there in five minutes.'

He switched off his 'Taxi' light and

put his foot down. Now he was the one weaving in and out between the cars. He was the one tapping on the steering wheel when he had to stop at the lights.

But he didn't feel stressed – he felt excited. A very famous person! He couldn't wait to find out who it was!

· CHAPTER 3 ·

Cab-driver Jack drove up to The Ritz hotel. There were crowds of fans on the pavement outside. There were photographers with big cameras. They must have heard that the very famous person was staying there. They must be waiting for him to come out.

The police had put up some barriers to hold the crowds back. Jack parked outside the hotel. The very famous person came out.

It was Harry Potter! The one from the films!

When the crowd saw him, they pushed and screamed. They burst through the barriers. Harry Potter broke into a run. He jumped into the taxi just in time. Jack put his foot down, and they screeched off up the road. The fans tried to run after the taxi, but they couldn't keep up.

'Phew!' said cab-driver Jack. 'That was scary!'

'You get used to it,' laughed Harry Potter.

Jack looked in his rear-view mirror. The famous round glasses glinted back at him. Then he saw something else in his rear-view mirror. The press photographers had got on their motorbikes. They were coming after Jack's taxi.

Harry Potter saw them too. 'Here we go!' he said, cheerfully.

The motorbikes came right up behind the taxi. They tried to ride along beside it. Jack's heart was pounding. He knew that he had to stay in front of them – if he let them overtake, they could force him to stop.

He didn't give the motorbikes room to ride beside the taxi. But he knew he wouldn't be able to hold them off for ever. He needed a plan.

Cab drivers know every side street and back alley off by heart. Jack decided to duck down a short cut and try to get away. But just before he reached the turning, he had to stop at a red light

The photographers jumped off their bikes and crowded round the taxi. Some girls crossing the road saw them. They ran between the cars to see who was inside the taxi. They spotted the famous round glasses.

'It's Harry Potter!' they shrieked.

People stopped crossing the road and ran over. They peered into the back of the taxi. They pressed their faces against the

windows. They tried to open the doors. Some people shouted at Jack.

'Open the doors!' they yelled.

At last, the lights turned to green, but Jack's taxi was blocked in by the crowd. He couldn't start moving in case he ran someone over. He couldn't stay where he was because the crowd might break his windows or dent his doors.

Harry Potter saw that Jack was worried. He said, 'Just start off slowly. They'll soon move out the way.'

So cab-driver Jack started slowly, but the crowd hardly moved. The car drivers behind were getting cross. They honked their horns. They opened their windows and shouted. Jack's cab with its very famous passenger was causing a big traffic jam.

Now cab-driver Jack was starting to feel really stressed.

'Keep calm, keep polite!' he told himself.

If he could just turn off the main road he might be able to lose the crowds. But the crowd was growing bigger and bigger and the taxi was completely stuck.

'Keep calm, keep polite!' said cab-driver Jack.

He looked at the clock. The minutes were ticking away. How could he get Harry Potter to the Film of the Year Show in time? The show was about to begin, and they were nowhere near the cinema.

'We're going to be late,' Jack said. 'I don't know what to do.'

Harry Potter didn't seem to be bothered about it at all. In fact, he seemed definitely cheerful.

'I think it's time to stop pretending,' he declared. He took off his famous round glasses. He took off his hair – it was a wig! He ruffled up his real hair, which was light sandy brown.

Jack gasped. His passenger didn't look

36

like Harry Potter at all any more. He was
not Harry Potter! He was a fake!

The people crowding around looked
as shocked as cab-driver Jack. The
photographers stopped taking pictures.
They pulled back and Jack was able to

drive away at last.

'What's going on?' asked Jack.

The boy in the back said, 'I'm a Harry Potter look-alike. When the real one's got to be somewhere important like the Film of the Year Show, the fans get to hear about it. Then they can mob him and stop him getting where he needs to be on time. So he sends me out first and everyone chases after me instead.'

Jack thought that was very clever.

'Who are you really then?' he said.

'My name's Adam. I'm a drama student,' said the passenger. 'Sorry I didn't tell you before. I wanted to see if I could make you think I was Harry Potter too.'

Adam asked cab-driver Jack to take him back to the hotel. He wanted to change

back into his own clothes and put his
Harry Potter things away until the next
time.

It didn't take long to get back to the
hotel now that they weren't surrounded by
photographers and fans. Adam got out and
came to the driver's window to pay.

'Sorry I tricked you,' he said.

'Don't worry about it,' said Jack.

He watched Adam go into the hotel. Then he pulled slowly out on to the road again. He turned his 'Taxi' light on to show that he didn't have any passengers.

'Getting stuck in a traffic jam was stressful,' he thought. 'But I did keep calm and polite.'

He felt pleased with himself but also a bit worn out. He needed a rest! He decided to go back to Paddington Station and wait in the line for a while. He was just pulling away when he saw a red-faced man in a suit striding towards him. He was wearing very shiny shoes and carrying a black briefcase.

The man stepped off the pavement. He stuck his hand out.

'Taxi! Taxi!' he shouted.

· CHAPTER 4 ·

'Ten Downing Street,' snapped the red-faced man. 'And be quick about it. I'm the Minister for Very Important Things and I've got a meeting with the Prime Minister!'

What a bossy-boots! He didn't even say please! Jack was annoyed, but he told himself, 'Keep calm, keep polite.' He turned off the 'Taxi' light to show that he had a passenger. Then he pulled out into the traffic again.

There were cars and buses on all sides.

They were pushing in. They were tooting their horns. There were traffic lights and crossings. Cab-driver Jack did not get stressed about having to stop at the lights but the passenger in the back did. He leaned forward. He muttered, 'Come on, Driver! Come on!'

'Can't you go any faster?' grumbled the red-faced man. 'The Prime Minister will not be happy if I keep him waiting!'

The pavements were full of people rushing along. Sometimes, someone tried to cross the busy road and all the drivers had to slam on their brakes. Cab-driver Jack did not get stressed about having to slam on the brakes, but the passenger did.

'What do these stupid people think they are doing?' he cried. He shook his fist at them. 'Run them over, I say!'

Jack quietly switched off the intercom. He could still see the red-faced man in his mirror, but at least he didn't have to listen to him any more.

At last, they reached number ten, Downing Street. There was a policeman standing outside, just like on the News. The red-faced man got out. He was in a terrible hurry.

'I'm late now,' he grumbled, as he handed over the money. 'I told you I was in a hurry, but it still took you ages to get me here. You are a rotten taxi driver!'

'Keep calm, keep polite!' Jack told himself, as he took the money.

'Thank you very much, sir,' he said brightly. 'I hope your meeting goes well!'

The Minister for Very Important things
scowled at Jack and stomped off towards
the famous front door. Jack was glad to see
the back of him.

'What a rude passenger!' he thought.
'But I did keep calm and polite.'

He felt very pleased with himself. He

had dealt with the two things that stressed taxi drivers out – being stuck in a traffic jam and having a rude passenger. He had told himself 'Keep calm, keep polite!' and it really did work. But hold on a minute – weren't there three things? What was the third one? Jack couldn't remember.

But when Jack checked his rear view mirror ready to drive away, he saw something glinting in the sun. It was the silver buckle on the Minister's black briefcase. He had forgotten to take it with him and it was leaning against the back seat on the floor. That was the third thing! People forgetting to take their belongings with them.

'Excuse me, sir,' Jack called across to him. 'You've forgotten your briefcase.'

The Minister for Very Important Things came back to the cab, looking cross. He flung open the door and grabbed his briefcase. But he didn't say thank you. He told Jack off!

'You should clean your taxi out,' he said. 'Look what was under my briefcase – a filthy, smelly old rag!'

He turned and marched away again in disgust.

'Smelly old rag?' thought cab-driver Jack.

He looked over his shoulder, but he couldn't see any smelly old rag. He got out and opened the back door. Then he saw it. It was squashed flat from being under the bossy man's briefcase. But it wasn't a smelly old rag.

It was a cuddly duck. It was bald and

grey, with patches of faded yellow fluff. It had two flat feet, a ripped red beak and two black beady eyes. Jack tried to think where he had seen it before.

He remembered the first people he had given a ride to, the nice mum and dad who were in London for the day with their children, Mitch, Molly and Little Min. Little Min had something tucked under her arm when they got into the taxi. When they got out, she didn't.

That must have been why she suddenly started crying. It wasn't because she was upset the taxi ride was over, like her dad said. She was upset because she didn't have her cuddly duck.

When someone left something in a taxi the driver had to decide whether it was

important enough to try and get it back to
them. Was a cuddly duck that looked more
like a smelly old rag important?

'Yes,' thought cab-driver Jack. 'Little Min
loves her duck and she'll probably keep
crying until she gets it back again.'

He sat the duck in the middle of the
back seat. He turned his 'Taxi' light off

because he had a passenger! Then he drove
back to the Natural History Museum as
fast as he could.

'Have you seen a family with a baby
in a buggy who wouldn't stop crying?' he
asked the woman at the desk.

'Yes,' she said. 'The baby was making such a racket we had to ask them to leave.'

'Oh no!' thought Jack. He tried to remember where they had said they were going to next. It was the Tower of London! He got back into his taxi and set off again.

As soon as he got to the Tower of London, he heard Min screaming. There were lots of people standing around. Jack grabbed the duck and pushed his way through the crowds towards the noise. Then he saw the family.

Little Min was wriggling and yelling so much that her mum could hardly hold on to her. Mitch and Molly were standing next to a beefeater and their dad was trying to take a photo of them.

'Smile,' he said. 'And could you all take

your hands off your ears?'

Jack went straight over to Little Min and gave her the duck. She stopped crying instantly, as if someone had switched the sound off. A big grin spread over her tear-stained face. A big grin spread over everybody else's faces too.

'Thank you,' said her mum. She squeezed Jack's arm.

'Thank you,' said her dad. He shook Jack's hand.

'How can we ever thank you enough?' they said.

They wanted to take Jack out for tea or at least buy him the best ice-cream that money could buy. Jack was tempted, but he shook his head.

'I'm sorry,' he said, 'but I can't hang around here. There's somewhere else I really need to be.'

Cab-driver Jack drove off again. But he didn't go back to Paddington Station. He drove out of the city. He went past shops and housing estates and factories. He came all the way back to the car supermarket, and pulled up outside the workshop at the back.

· CHAPTER 5 ·

Jack jumped out of the taxi and ran across the yard. He wasn't allowed in the workshop so he went to the door and called out.

'Uncle Archie! Uncle Archie!'

Brian appeared from under the Escort.

'Hello, young Jack,' he said. 'Archie's in the stores.'

The stores were a couple of dark poky rooms at the back of the workshop. They were lined with shelves full of cardboard boxes. Jack found Uncle Archie sorting through them with a clip-board.

'Uncle Archie,' he said. 'Please can you take me home?'

Uncle Archie's mouth fell open. He was amazed. Car-mad Jack, wanting to go home, when he could be playing in the cars at the car supermarket? What was going on?

'Aren't you feeling well?' he said.

'I'm feeling fine,' Jack said. 'I don't want to go home and stay there. I just need to pop

in for a few minutes.'

Uncle Archie shrugged.

'OK,' he said, rubbing his chin. 'I suppose I will need to take Sam's taxi out for a test run before we start working on it, and your house would be just the right sort of distance.'

Jack grinned.

'Thanks, Uncle Archie. You're the best!' he said.

Jack sat in the back of the taxi. Uncle Archie drove. They had the intercom on so that they could talk to each other. Uncle Archie wanted to know why Jack had to go home. Had he forgotten something?

'No,' Jack told him. 'I was pretending I had a family in my taxi and the toddler lost her cuddly duck. Well, Nico lost Crocky this morning, and when I was playing I suddenly had an idea where Crocky might be.'

As soon as they pulled up outside Jack's house, he jumped out. Uncle Archie kept the engine running. He opened the bonnet to see if he could work out why it was over-heating.

Jack ran round the back of the house. He could hear Nico sobbing through the sitting room window. Mum was sitting on the kitchen step. She looked fed up.

'Jack!' she said, jumping up. 'What are you doing home? What's wrong? Are you ill?'

'No, I just had an idea,' he said.

Jack slipped past Mum and went into the sitting room. Mum's knitting bag was leaning against the settee. When they had searched for Crocky, Jack had looked under the settee, but he had not moved Mum's knitting bag. He moved it now.

And there was Crocky! Mum must have put her knitting bag down on top of him without noticing he was there. Now he was squashed down flat, looking very sorry for himself. Jack grabbed him and plumped him up a bit. Then he gave him to Nico.

'Clocky!' cried Nico.

He was as happy as a pig in a puddle.

Jack was happy too. He ran back outside. Uncle Archie was just shutting the bonnet of the taxi.

'I've found out what the problem is now,' said Uncle Archie. 'And how about you? Did you find Crocky?'

Jack nodded.

'You'll be everyone's favourite person for the rest of the day then!' chuckled Uncle Archie.

By the time they got back to the car supermarket Brian was ready for a doughnut break. It was a sunny day, so they brought some chairs out into the yard. They sat in the sunshine, munching their way through a big bag of mixed doughnuts.

When they had finished, Brian drove the taxi into the workshop so that he could start work on it. 'What shall I do now?' thought Jack. He usually made a poster of the cars he played in. Dad said Jack's posters sold more cars than he did! But the taxi was not for sale.

Jack decided to do some drawing anyway. He ran over to the showroom to fetch his pens and paper. He used one of the chairs outside the workshop as a table and knelt down in the sunshine to draw.

Jack drew a picture of the taxi. He wrote beside it:

Please do not leeve your things in the back of this taxi. For eksample, no breefcases or ducks.

Then he drew little pictures of a briefcase

and a cuddly duck and put red crosses over them.

He was just sitting back on his heels to admire his drawing when Sam and Uncle Archie came striding into the yard. They had to wait for Brian to finish working on the taxi so they came over to talk to Jack.

'Nice drawing!' Sam said. 'I've got a

notice in my cab about not leaving your things behind, but no one seems to see it. I need something more unusual. Something like this would do the trick!'

Jack held out his picture.

'You can have it if you like,' he said.

Sam was delighted. 'What a brilliant present!' he said. 'I'll stick it over the top of the old notice. But what can I give you in return?'

Jack grinned. 'You've already given me the best present in the world,' he said. 'You've let me play in your taxi!'

Uncle Archie ruffled Jack's hair.

'They don't call him Car-mad Jack for nothing!' he said.

Look out for more of Car-mad Jack's adventures in the following books:

The Speedy Sports Car
The Versatile Van
The Motorbike in the Mountains
The Marvellous Minibus
The Rugged Off-roader